Love Sean n Rach

Requests for permission to make copies of any part of this work
should be mailed to: Permissions Department,
Harcourt Brace and Company, 6277 Sea Harbor Drive,
Orlando, Florida 32887-6777.

First published in Great Britain in 1995 by Andersen Press Ltd.
First U.S. edition 1996

Gulliver Green is a registered trademark of Harcourt Brace & Company.

Library of Congress Cataloging-in-Publication Data
Grindley, Sally.
Peter's place / by Sally Grindley; illustrated by
Michael Foreman.—1st U.S. ed.
p.   cm.
"A Gulliver Green book."
Summary: Peter helps clean up the disaster when an oil tanker spills its
cargo on his shoreline, but only time will truly heal the place.
ISBN 0-15-200916-7
[1. Oil spills—Fiction. 2. Pollution—Fiction.] I. Foreman, Michael,
1938–   ill. II. Title. III. Series.
PZ7.G88446Pe 1996/ [Fic]—dc20   95-5820

A B C D E

Printed in Italy

Gulliver Green® Books focus on various aspects of ecology and the envi-
ronment, and a portion of the proceeds from the sale of these books will
be donated to protect, preserve, and restore native forests.

Printed and bound in Italy by Grafiche AZ, Verona

PETER'S
PLACE

PETER'S PLACE

Sally Grindley

ILLUSTRATED BY

Michael Foreman

A GULLIVER GREEN BOOK

HARCOURT BRACE & COMPANY

San Diego   New York   London

This was Peter's place. All along the wind-torn beaches, all the way up the ravaged cliff face, this land's end was full of life.

Guillemots, shags, kittiwakes, eider ducks, and long-tailed ducks screeched and squawked and gossiped to one another while in the turbulent ocean below, seals and otters bobbed and weaved and played and feasted on the sea's riches.

Some came here to have their young. Others lived here year-round.

They did not notice the distant procession of tankers. They were snug in their haven.

Peter came here to skim stones across the wave tops. He came here to search for crabs among tide pools. He came here to throw bread for the ducks and fish for the seals.

The eider ducks were Peter's favorites. They knew his call. They were not afraid of him. They knew this was his place, too. He brought them food, and they waddled over to greet him, each fighting to get a bite, though Peter made sure that none of them ever missed out.

But one night there was an accident, and Peter's place was changed. A passing oil tanker drew too close. Too close for the comfort of the playful seals; too close for the comfort of the cooing eiders; too close to miss the rocks that lay just below the rough tide.

Too close to Peter's place.

The scream of tons of metal smashing onto the rocks alerted the nearby farmers and jolted Peter from his sleep. They ran to the cliff's edge and watched as the tanker broke apart on the rocks.

Fearing for their lives, the men on board the sinking ship were lifted away, leaving the tanker to fight its own battle. From deep inside its belly a foul-smelling blackness spread into the night.

When morning came, the slick blackness was everywhere. The waves frothed black, the once-silver sands oozed black, and every crevice of the jagged rocks was filled with black.

Peter scrambled down the cliff and stood where he had stood so often before.

A young seal bobbed, shivering, in the sea. Its once soft, gray fur, now matted with oil, could no longer hold in its body's warmth.

Each new wave that crashed onto the shore delivered more dying creatures to Peter's place.

A guillemot plucked furiously at its matted feathers, poisoning itself. The oil kept it from flying. An eider duck flailed about, trying to move, and then lay motionless, weakened by its struggle.

Peter walked quietly over to it. He didn't want to frighten it. It was frightened enough. But the duck knew his call.

Peter picked up the duck.
It rested its head against Peter's
chest while he cradled it in his
arms, his silent tears dried by
the wind.

Then gentle hands took Peter's
duck from him and carried it
away to be cleaned and looked
after. He heard his father urging
him to join in with the rescue.

For many days he helped hose and scrub away the sticky slime that covered every rock and filled every niche.

Day by day, month by month, the ocean and rain and wind helped wash Peter's place, too.

This is Peter's place now. When his duck waddles over to take bread from his hands, Peter marvels at its survival, and he smiles at its family sliding and tripping over the rocks.

And sometimes, when he picks up a stone to skip across the tops of the waves, his hands are left sticky and black, and the memories come rushing back.

For, not far below the surface, in little nooks and crannies, between the rocks, under the sand, are ugly black scars that can never be washed away.

But this is still Peter's place. All along the wind-torn beaches, all the way up the ravaged cliff face, this land's end is full of life.